The House on Deer-Track Trail

The House on Deer-Track Trail

by MARTY KELLY

illustrated by RONALD HIMLER

McGraw-Hill Book Company
New York : St. Louis : San Francisco : Auckland : Düsseldorf : Johannesburg : Kuala Lumpur :
London : Mexico : Montreal : New Delhi : Panama : Paris : São Paulo : Singapore : Sydney :
Tokyo : Toronto

Library of Congress Cataloging in Publication Data

Kelly, Marty.
  The house on Deer Track Trail.

  SUMMARY: The animals' existence in the abandoned old house is
threatened when a young couple appears and talks about redoing the
place.
  I. Himler, Ronald. II. Title.
PZ7.K2965Ho   [Fic]   75-41455
ISBN 0-07-033886-8
ISBN 0-07-033887-6 lib. bdg.

Book Design by Lynn Braswell

  2 3 4 5 6 R A B P 7 8 9 8 7 6

For Peggy, Marty, and Budd;
my best friends

One

THE old house had been boarded up and abandoned long ago. Hardly anybody even remembered it was there. Tall and faded, it stood almost hidden by a grove of cottonwood trees. Halfway up the coulee, behind the house, empty barns leaned gently toward the meadow with its deep, wild flowers. Once in a while a lone cowboy jogged past on his pony, checking the fences, but that was all. So the old place settled down among the wild geraniums and gradually went to sleep. As the years went by a board blew off here. A window broke there. Grass grew up through the front steps and the old house snoozed softly—softly—

Then along came this snoopy packrat. He had been living out of doors in the good, clean mountain air, eating seeds and grain and leftover camper's scraps, forever on the move. Now, most pack-rats are content to live in barns or sheds or any old outbuilding corner, but not this packrat. He stuck his head through a hole in the wall of the boarded-up house and peeked around. It was dim and private and sheltered from the wind. Packy had found his place. He stepped right in and made himself comfortable. The old house barely knew he was there.

In the course of time, other creatures came to visit and some remained. Chk, a friendly gray squirrel, climbed in through the broken upstairs window. Skeet, the neighborhood skunk, shared the house on damp days. Little Green Grass Snake slipped inside during a rainstorm because she was afraid of thunder. A whole colony of spiders occupied the downstairs front room. They were shy and didn't care for the daylight, so they draped their web from the settee to the ceiling and the pictures on the wall, and they were snug in their secret abode.

Paper shell wasps hung a nest behind the ancient stove in the kitchen, among the pots and pans. Their's was a private entrance, through a small, dislodged windowpane close by. And in the attic, a grouchy hoot-owl took up residence. He was old and practically blind. They were not afraid of him.

It didn't take Packy long to discover the green apple tree down behind the slanting horse barn. He liked nothing better than chawing green apples. He splashed the juice and sucked on the core, making a terribly moisty noise, then picked out the seeds and nibbled them daintily.

Occasionally he trotted over to the beaver dam in the meadow to call on Benny Beaver, an industrious fellow who lived in a house built of faggots and mud right in the middle of the stream. He gossiped with the field mice and the little foxes in the woods and nodded to the green frogs, keeping track of things.

On pure white nights, Lonesome Coyote pointed his chin at the moon and yipped for joy. Then the meadow was bathed in brightness and the wild deer came bounding down the twisted mountain trail to prance and leap in the clearing. With the first bird chirp, they raced back up the mountain, leaving only their hoofprints among the mushrooms.

Lonesome Coyote once tried to eat Packy but Packy put up such a scrap, he decided to befriend him instead. The wily coyote lived in a cave among the rocks where he could look down at the house on the deer-track trail.

In the house, the inhabitants got along very well, attending one another with courtesy and respect. Packy raced from hiding place to hiding place, happily cacheing little trinkets he favored. Chk sociably relayed news back and forth while gathering seed pods and nuts for winter. Little Green Grass Snake timidly kept out of everyone's way, just grateful for friendship and a corner inside. Skeet went confidently where he pleased without bothering the others.

All this coming and going was not unpleasant to the old house. It dozed, waking now and then to listen awhile, then relapsed contentedly into half-slumber. The small creatures were no trouble at all. It was a splendid arrangement until this morning. Packy awoke with a start.

What was that!

He sat up, straining his ears. Then he scrambled from his bed and raced to the chink in the wall where he could scan the whole front yard. His cowlick stood up straight and his nose twitched irritably as he spied a cream-colored station wagon carefully creeping over the rose bushes and wild geraniums, toward the front gate.

Packy dashed upstairs. A quick patter on the roof outside let him know Chk, the gray squirrel, was watching, too.

"Looks like company," Chk whispered through the torn screen.

"They've got a nerve!" Packy ex-

ploded. He whisked outside to join Chk under the leaves of the big cottonwood tree that stretched across the roof.

A young man and woman stepped from the car and entered the yard through the overgrown gateway. They picked their path from the front where Lilac grew thick and shaggy to the back where Virginia Creeper hid the sparrows' nests and shaded the back porch. Packy and Chk followed, running along the rooftop curiously.

"This is really lovely," the woman exclaimed. "Why would anyone exchange this grand old mansion for that little cottage down the road?" and the man laughed.

"This house is a shambles. Grandfather built it almost a century ago when pioneers raised big families. Nobody wants an old horror like this nowadays."

He pointed out the loose boards, the sagging roof and many other signs of neglect.

"No one has lived here for years. Even the floors are unsafe. That little house is more suitable for us, and close to the road, too. We have plenty of time to build a more spacious place later on. This old relic will never do."

"But I LIKE this house. It has a beautiful view and so much room. Why don't we restore it?"

She stepped carefully onto the porch.

"How about that!" Packy snapped.

He and Chk dashed inside and raced to their spy holes in the wall.

"Better let me go first," the man warned, tugging at the rusty latch on the door.

The old house gave a little gasp of surprise.

Sudden rays of sunshine sent the spider colony fleeing for cover, all except Grand-daddy. He hunched in a corner of the web and squinted while his timid daughters herded their frightened young ones into the shadows.

Little dust puffs followed the people across the faded carpet. Packy watched from his vantage point where seeping rain had spoiled the sprigged wall paper and left the plaster weakened. It suited him to a T. He could see anywhere in the whole house and guard his treasures at the same time.

"Look at these wonderful antiques!" exclaimed the woman.

Packy looked. He saw his worn horse-hair sofa with its springs upthrust and cover split. He saw the ugly pictures against the sunless walls, murky with age. A startled field mouse darted from a corner squeaking in fright as it disappeared from sight. The woman sprang back.

In the vast, cool kitchen stood an old-fashioned harvest table with smooth benches on either side and a pine dry sink. There was a cookstove, and beside it a woodbox still held a few cottonwood chocks and cedar sticks. A cricket sang inside the oven and little dust moats slid down a sunbeam.

"This place is stale," the man murmured.

"This place is a museum!" the woman cried in delight. "We could do it over and have a palace."

The man sputtered, "You don't really mean that!"

He spied the thin gray wasp's nest behind the stove and recognized the sound of wasps at work. The woman tapped her foot and murmured, "Yes, I think this will be the family room," and she moved back toward the porch, out of the dust. The man followed, sneezing forlornly.

"Well, I guess I'd better get a contractor up here to see what can be done," and he tugged the front door shut behind him.

Packy's heart leaped to his throat. His house! They would be rummaging around in his house, tearing his things apart, exposing his treasures!

"What do you know about that!" he exploded to Chk, and his long tail whipped the dust angrily as he ran back inside the walls and up to the roof to watch the people return to their car and drive carefully back across the seedling trees and rose bushes. A meadow lark flew up and scolded as they passed. Lilac rustled in dismay. And the old house mumbled to itself.

Two

PACKY drummed on the window-sill with his hind legs. Chk sat beside him, and they stuffed themselves fiercely on dried corn from the old seed bag in the attic.

"Why do you suppose they want to

move in here?" Chk asked, as he flipped his fluffy tail excitedly.

"There's plenty of room for everybody if they would leave us alone, but you know how people are—always changing things around, messing things up!" Packy fretted. Abruptly he bade good-bye to Chk and ran back inside through the broken upstairs window with the tattered screen. Chk saw some crows in a nearby Box Elder tree, and he hastened over to tell them about the people.

Packy got busy. There was no time to waste. He went to his cache in the woodbox where he fondled his treasures: a blue glass marble, an assortment of buttons, a sewing machine bobbin and two buffalo nickels. Then he snatched his favorite, the marble, and chased off through the maze in the walls. All day long, he went back and forth, making a million little footprints on the way. He changed all his hiding places and it was so much fun, he changed them all over again.

In no time alarm spread among the creatures on the deer-track trail. The crows, natural gossips, told everyone, and soon Packy saw Skeet Skunk come ambling through a gap in the foundation, his little black eyes bright with sympathy.

Packy brushed back a wisp of limp hair and told him the bad news.

"We'll see about that!" Skeet promised with a threatening wave of his tail.

Then Little Green, the grass snake, slipped in to see if she could be of any help. Packy barely had time to talk to her.

"I don't know what you could do. You're too small, any way you look at it. I am much too upset to talk," and he disappeared with the last button in his mouth. Little Green flicked her tongue and slid into a corner to wait for the harassed pack-rat to return.

Down the side of the bluff in the meadow, Lonesome Coyote trotted cautiously, looking this way and that. He reached the sagging front gate and stood there, grinning. Chk, for once unafraid, leaned from the gingerbread trimming under the eaves and told him the story. He stopped grinning.

"That's too bad," Lonesome Coyote muttered. "Packy likes that place so much. Personally I couldn't stand being cooped up. Maybe we can frighten the people away." And he sat on his haunches grinning thoughtfully. At last he got up and trotted off toward his bluff, tail drooping.

The wasps in the kitchen were all for attacking at once. The idea of anybody expecting to remove their beautiful paper-shell which had been so hard to make in the first place. The very idea!

A mean little hobo weasel stuck his head into the house and called out, "Any-

body home? Heard you folks might be needing some help," but Packy sent him on his way. Nobody liked Weasel, especially Packy. He bared his teeth and the hair bristled on his neck.

Weasel ducked his head back outside and snapped, "You don't have to get so huffy. I know how you feel. Oh, well," and he slipped into the brush after a quick look-around.

The crows must have told the owl in the attic, for he thumped and banged all day long, making a dreadful racket, hooting angrily to himself and anybody who would listen.

Packy was beginning to scheme furiously. He made a fast run to the beaver dam and called out to Mr. Beaver. The fat friendly beaver came swimming to the grassy bank where Packy stood, dipping up cold water and sucking it from his fingers.

"Did you call?" he asked. Ben Beaver was the busiest creature alive and he didn't care to be disturbed at work, but a friend in need was something else.

Packy had to shout to make himself heard. The wind always whispers secrets to the reeds in the beaver dams and the listening grass sings out, "Sh-sh-sh-" whenever someone is near. So Packy shouted, "Yes, I called you, Ben."

The beaver climbed up the grassy bank beside him. He made himself comfortable and suggested, "Not so loud, if you please."

Packy told him about the strangers in the house and Ben murmured from time to time, "A pity!" As Packy speculated on one idea then another, Ben nodded his head.

"Well, there's one thing I can do, if it comes to it," and he mentioned a daring plan.

Packy stared at him for a minute then replied, "Well, I'm not sure, but maybe. Just maybe."

Ben nodded again.

"Well—just let me know if I can be of any help. But isn't it a shame!"

Packy thanked him hastily and took off for home. He was beginning to feel more cheerful. Ben watched good-naturedly, then slid back into the clear, cool water and swam away.

A few nights later, during a sudden thunderstorm, Packy was astonished to hear the station wagon stop outside the gate again. The man and woman dashed from the car and into the house while thunder peeled wildly. Somewhere a big tree cracked and split in two. The woman listened fearfully to the awesome sound. The man lit a lantern and carried two sleeping bags into the house. Then the woman unpacked a knapsack with sandwiches, deviled eggs and fresh peaches while the man uncorked a thermos of hot coffee.

Packy forgot his fury at the unexpected aroma. He began to sniff eagerly. It smelled great. He inched closer, and Chk, who had been sleeping, flipped his tail rapidly and woke up.

"Chk! Chk!" he exclaimed. The woman turned. The man laughed and said it was only the wind. He was hungry.

They laid a picnic cloth on a card table and sat down on folding camp chairs by lantern light.

"Isn't this romantic," the woman laughed and Packy thought so, too. While they ate, lightning flashed and the storm rolled itself away toward the distant hills. A few wandering raindrops splattered and dripped from the big tree beside the porch, and the small creatures of the house sat quietly in the shadows and waited.

When the people finished, they wrapped the scraps in paper and tossed them into the woodbox. They replaced the extra food in the knapsack and left it on the card table. Then they unrolled the sleeping bags, blew out the lantern and went to sleep. Soon the house was still, but it was listening. The wind quieted.

The small residents remained where they were for awhile. When the people were sleeping soundly, Packy dashed to the scraps in the woodbox and shook them out. What a feast!

He climbed inside the knapsack and kicked out some sugar cookies and oranges which Skeet couldn't devour fast enough. He sat in the pitch dark, holding the oranges with his tiny paws and sucked them greedily.

The timid spiders slid down their ropes and skittered across the table, gathering crumbs. Chk carried a cooky through the walls, out across the wet roof and onto the outstretched arm of the big cottonwood tree. There he hid the cooky and raced back so fast, not one raindrop touched him.

Ransacking the woman's handbag, Packy discovered a shiny jeweled lipstick. Out of the bag it went, and into his hiding place behind the stairs. He replaced it with a treasured sardine can key.

The small friends were so busy feasting and inspecting their guests, morning streaked across the sky before they knew it. The man awoke, stretched his arms, and yawned like a lion. It frightened the spiders back into the shadows. Everyone else stopped and waited.

The woman awoke, smiled and climbed from her sleeping bag. Slipping her foot into her shoe, she screamed shrilly and flung it from her. It fell to the floor. So did Little Green. She had been comfortably curled inside.

The woman was terribly upset. So was Little Green. She swished outside to the tall grass with her little tongue flipping angrily.

"She almost killed me. I didn't even touch her," and she raced away. In the confusion, the foolish owl in the attic fell off his perch and flapped his wings frantically trying to regain his place. He hooted and screeched and all the household were alarmed. He had never carried on like this before. He knocked aside several picture frames and broke a looking glass before he settled down and went fast asleep.

The man said, "Let's go back to the cottage for breakfast. You are too upset. We can return later to discuss any changes to be made."

They hurried to the car through a shower of dew and drove away. The old house watched, feeling cranky. Lilac trembled beside the gate.

Three

ACKY was still snickering at the way Little Green had frightened the woman as he approached the sleeping bag and spied the zipper. He picked at it, then tugged at it. Chk joined him. Chk discovered the trick of sliding the latch up and down. They were gleefully jiggling it when Chk felt a tug at his tail. He chattered and squeaked, trying to get loose, but it held him fast. The more he pulled, the more it hurt. He was breathless with fright. Packy gnawed his hands and worried the zipper. There! Chk was free!

He scolded furiously and sprang for a hole in the wall, his tail still smarting. Once on the roof, in the sunshine, he crimped his tail a couple of times. His beautiful tail! He wasn't going near that thing again.

Packy chewed the zipper but he could not get it off. Many times during the morning, he returned to the puzzle only to meet defeat. In his irritation, he gobbled the entire supply of green apples he had hidden behind the stairs.

That afternoon, the people returned laden with brooms, buckets and mops. They began taking the pictures down from the walls.

"Whew!" the woman gasped, "there are a million spiders in this place!" Then a scared baby spider ran up her arm and she dropped a large oil painting to the floor, shattering the heavy frame against her toe. The woman cried out, hopping back and forth, holding her throbbing foot.

The man helped with the remaining pictures. They carried them outside and leaned them against the porch railing, in full sunshine. Then the woman limped back inside and dragged forth the old settee with great determination. It was very heavy . . . On to the kitchen she went, her dust cloth swishing.

All this time, the inhabitants of the house remained behind the walls, peering anxiously back and forth. They darted from one peephole to the next, sometimes making a noise which caused the woman to stare at the ceiling and wonder. The old house stared boldly back at her.

In the kitchen she began to push things out of her way. The man had forgotten the wasp's nest, and the wasps went about their own business. They buzzed a little louder. Then she heard them. Investigating the threatening hum, she brushed against the delicate hive. It dashed to the floor and split on the spot. The wasps poured out.

As she turned to run, three wasps caught her and stung her hard. The rest buzzed angrily through the air, making short circles overhead until the room seemed to be filled with the sound and feel of them.

The woman stumbled into the dining room, swatting left and right, shouting wildly. She tripped and fell and was stung again before she could slam the creaky old kitchen door. Dust filled the air. The woman jumped up sneezing and crying and ran right into the man who had been examining the foundation outside. He dragged her to the creek where he splashed her with cold water and mud, at which she wept all the louder. Her hair hung limply and her face swelled from the stings. In their wet clothes, the people both looked discouraged.

Once more they got into their car and went off to the cottage to nurse their wounds. The woman was still wailing as they swept out of sight, and Packy let his breath out slowly. He was upset, too. What a fuss!

Chk was hiding among the leaves, afraid to show his face. The house in the coulee fell to brooding. The upstairs owl must have been frightened out of his wits, for he didn't make a sound. He just scrooched down on his shaky perch, and his staring eyes never blinked. Now and then, he flicked his head as though annoyed, but he didn't utter one sound. After awhile, he went to sleep.

By this time, Skeet, who happened by,

managed to unzip the cover on the knapsack. Chk, who had been watching, slid
inside and dragged forth some candy bars
with chocolate and lots of nuts. Delightful!
Skeet grumbled because there were no
more oranges, and he tore the candy
wrappers into shreds. Chk found a package
of chewing gum and he dropped this to
Skeet who had a good time loosening all
the sticks and eating them, one by one.
Then he waddled outside and down the
trail.

The afternoon drifted away with
Packy and Chk sitting on the rooftop in
the blessed quiet.

Lonesome Coyote, watching from his
cave in the rocks, had heard all the
commotion and he shrank within his skin.
No wonder Packy didn't want people to
move into his house. There would be no
peace in the meadow at all.

That night, he stood on the point of

rocks and howled and howled and yipped and yipped. Down in the cottage, the man stepped outside to listen. He liked the sound of coyotes at night, but his wife called, "For goodness sake! Close that door before those wild animals come right inside with us!"

The man grinned and returned to the cottage. He asked, "Do you really want to restore that old place? You know, some contractors are coming up here this weekend to look over the job. If you change your mind, now is the time. I think you should," but the woman shook her head. She still liked the house. She planned to go back, first thing in the morning, sore face and all, and start moving the furniture.

The man sighed and Lonesome Coyote looked up at the stars and resumed his terrible, savage cry. It came hurtling back from the mountains, and it sounded like coyotes on every point for miles around. The inhabitants of the house on the deer-track trail were filled with admiration and lulled by its force. The woman in the little house down the road shivered.

Lilac, beside the gate, whispered softly to the bird's nest in her branches, and the old house hugged itself quietly and rocked to and fro.

Four

ORNING. Packy lay curled
among his treasures. Chk hunched on a
branch of the great cottonwood tree and
snacked on his cooky. Skeet slept peace-
fully in the grass-grown manger of the
tumble-down horsebarn, and the old owl,

returning after a night's foraging, swooped across the windowsill in the attic, grumbling to himself. Yesterday he had barely had any sleep. Even the night moths with their big green eyes were deserting the attic as a result of the activity downstairs. The owl settled on his perch and gobbled in dissatisfaction before closing his big round eyes.

That day the man noisily began to pull off the boards covering the windows. Daylight flooded all through the house and this outraged Packy. He liked privacy.

The wasps had left the kitchen and were already busily building a new nest inside the barn.

When the woman started a fire in the stove, Chk retreated to the top of the giant cottonwood tree and refused to come into the house. Packy rather liked the fire. It was cozy. Many a summer morning had found him drenched with dew. He appreciated the extra warmth.

Then the woman carried a pail of water from the spring and started a pot of coffee. The fire must have startled the owl in the attic for he flapped his big wings and bumped around fiercely, trying to get comfortable. It was a most alarming disturbance, and the woman stopped her tasks to stare at the ceiling, listening intently. Her hands trembled as she picked up the stove poker and banged on the kitchen wall, shouting wildly at the owl. The man came running into the house, but when he saw her, they burst into gales of laughter.

It unnerved Packy completely. He tumbled through the hole in the wall, right into the bucket of spring water. Squeaking in terror, he swam around and around, swallowing great, choking mouthfuls. The man snatched the pail and tossed the water out the door, and Packy was off like a shot, dripping wet, teeth chattering, through the grass to the beaver dam. The head-splitting shrieks of the woman were ringing in his ears.

He yelled to Benny Beaver who came gliding toward him at once. Benny climbed up the bank beside Packy and told him to roll in the tall grass to dry his coat. A rest in the sun would finish the job.

"Well, how are you getting along with your people?" he asked sociably.

Packy snapped, limbs shaking with chill, "I've had it, Ben! I've just had it. The sooner we get rid of them, the better!" and he snuggled deep into the grass in the brave sunshine and fluffed his fur.

Ben nodded solemnly. The time had come.

When Packy worked up the courage to return home, he heard the woman bemoaning the loss of her lipstick. Sunshine streamed all through the house revealing the many cracks in the plaster, holes in the

walls and the seamy, stained wall paper. It was such a mess. The old house was silent in humiliation.

When the woman complained about it, the man chuckled and replied, "It's still not too late to cancel the whole thing. I like the little house down the road. This place will be snowbound in winter. We'll never get out until spring."

The woman stared at him thoughtfully.

Chk was nowhere in sight. Neither were the spiders. The wasps buzzed back and forth outside. They were much too busy to harbor a grudge. Across the meadow the crows flocked, calling a greeting to Packy as they flew off. Well, it was still his house. He ducked between the walls and proceeded to move his keepsakes to a corner behind the stairs.

The people rattled and pounded all day long, calling back and forth across the house. Upstairs the man pulled off a broken window screen. The frame was old and dry. It split in his hands. He threw down his tools and stalked from room to room, tapping on walls, inspecting joists and beams. It really was an old house. New paint! New plaster. Insulation and siding. Whew!

The old house shuddered in agreement.

Weasel, still hanging around in spite of himself, stuck his head up among the chips of the woodpile and startled the man chopping wood for the fire. Skeet terrified the woman by ambling right into the the kitchen, but the woman screeched so hard, Skeet turned around and waddled back outside and down the trail to the woods.

The noisy goings-on had Packy worn out. With a heavy heart, he curled into a little desolate ball on top of his trinkets and napped. The old house trembled wearily.

It was tired of confusion and it resented all the clutter.

The people cooked their supper on the stove and walked through the meadow at dusk. Wild flowers lingered on the threshold of the day, spreading their perfume. Down in the hollow, little green frogs piped, learning to croak. A catbird called from across the pond while the man skipped rocks across the darkening water. The woman admired the sunset and breathed deep of the rich scented air.

Lonesome Coyote stood on his ledge and watched them stroll the deer path in the meadow. Chk, racing through the trees at the edge of the woods, chattered his impudence, but the people didn't even hear him.

At length, they turned back to the house. Packy watched them get into the car and depart for the cottage for the night. Then he picked up his scrubby little legs and fairly flew across the field to the beaver dam where late blackbirds trilled among the cattails.

Benny Beaver joined him and together they struck out for the house on the deer-track trail. Lilac saw them coming before the others. She had grown a whole head taller in just one month. The old house perked up with interest.

Five

ACKY was anxious. He wrung his hands and got in Ben's way, but Ben was a patient creature. He didn't complain. He went right to work and he worked steadily all night long. The friends waited, even Little Green, who had heard the news and came happily back to watch the excitement.

Just before dawn, there was a sharp crack, then a tremendous roar. The great cottonwood tree which had stretched its wide arms across the front porch, crashed down upon the house. It went through the rooftree and smashed the attic window, knocking the sleepy, late-hunting owl right off his perch.

The old house trembled and braced itself. Boards dropped and splintered on all sides. The windows splattered and the great tree settled closer with renewed crackling of boughs.

Packy was expecting it, but even he was startled nearly out of his skin. Chk was nowhere to be seen, but bright eyes from all over the meadow stared in shocked surprise.

When the dust finally settled, everybody came timidly back to the yard. Not a word was spoken. Nobody was hurt. They had all been watching and waiting.

Packy, first, crept into the ruins to see

how bad things were. He could still make his way between the walls to his treasures. The roof was cracked and one broad branch went through, but it didn't matter. Things were pretty scrambled, but that didn't matter either. Chk and Skeet joined him inside and they looked around approvingly. Skeet said, "It's still as good as new," and Chk raced here and there, exploring for himself. The old house leaned back stoutly.

While they were inside, Ben yawned and stretched. His part was finished. The sun was up and birds were twittering in astonishment from fence posts and trees. Ben headed back toward the beaver dam.

Packy and Chk were examining the house from top to bottom when the cream-colored station wagon stopped at the gate. The man and woman sat as though stunned. At last the man said, "Well, let us get out and see what happened."

He discovered Ben's work and shook his head.

"Well, that's about the end of it. This house can never be repaired now. Guess we are lucky at that," and there was a briskness to his voice.

The woman drew a long breath and replied, "We are lucky to have the little cottage after all."

She sighed. And she looked back over her shoulder toward the ruins of the old house as they departed for good. The old house grinned a lop-sided grin.

Packy and his friends were overjoyed. The house was still home to them. There was plenty of room inside. Packy danced a leaping gavot on the rooftree and Chk chattered like mad.

The owl discovered he would have to land in the fallen cottonwood tree in order to climb inside, but this was even easier for him.

Old Man Coyote stood on his ledge and listened to the merriment. His ears were very keen this morning. Soon he

trotted off to the meadow in search of breakfast and a chase to keep his muscles in shape.

To make things perfect, the man returned a few days later to nail new boards across the downstairs windows. He told his wife, "I don't want any cattle or wild animals to get inside the house and fall through the floors."

Packy, his bright eyes gleaming, blinked from a hole in the plaster.

Now the house on the deer-track trail is quiet again. So quiet you can hear the sparrows chatter in the Virginia Creeper on the back porch and the wind whistle through the broken chimney. Cottonwood is already busily sending up a new shoot to look things over and replace the great tree outside. Lilac is blooming in a burst of radiance, completely covering the rickety front gate.

The old house shifts comfortably with a gigantic yawn and settles closer to earth. Ever so gently, it is going back to sleep.

Acknowledgment

Gratefully, I extend credit to the Honorable Robert J. Nelson, District Judge of the Eighth Judicial District of Cascade County, Montana. He is a knowledgeable man on packrats. With the same appreciation, I extend thanks to Squire Henry J. Cunningham of Sun River, Montana. His was the authority on beavers, generously supplied.

Marty Kelly